Finding God Through The Pain Of Divorce

GENA MICHELLE VEASEY

Contents

Dedication   1

Acknowledgements   3

Introduction   5

Part 1   7

Chapter 1   9

Self-Check: Be Honest With Yourself   14

Surrendering All   17

Self-Check: Be Honest With Yourself   22

Chapter 2   23

Self-Check: Be Honest With Yourself   32

Part 2   33

Chapter 3   35

Self-Check: Be Honest With Yourself   41

Part 3   43

Chapter 4   45

Self-Check: Be Honest With Yourself   52

Conclusion   55

Prayer Of Affirmation   59

Lessons Learned   61

This book is dedicated to those who are hurting, brokenhearted, and crushed in spirit by the pain of divorce. May you find strength during your time of trial, as the power of God surrounds you with peace and comfort.

Acknowledgements

I would like to acknowledge my parents Geneva Weaver and Leavy Riley for being by my side during every phase of my life. Thank you for your love and undying support.

To my God mother Ms. Willie Reid, you are truly God sent. Words will never express my gratitude for the role you play in my life. Thank you!

This book would have never been written if it weren't for my children, Altaron II, Natalie, Evan, and Donovan Veasey. I love you so much! Thank you for being the reason I had no choice but to keep waking up every day!

To my sisters, Tanisha Parker, Mrs. Angela Linsey, Mrs. Sylatha Taylor, and my sisters in Christ Mrs. Terrella Thomas, Yolonda Goodwine, Tammy Smith, Ms. Pamela Lewis, Mrs. Wanda Kimbrough, and Mrs. Michelle Clinkscales. Each of you contributed to my successful breakthrough from the pain of my divorce. Thank you for lifting me up when I didn't know which way was up. Thank you for your prayers, encouragement, sternness, support, and Godly counsel.

To my Publisher, Ms. Paula P., at Speak Life Publications, you and your staff are amazingly talented. Thank you so much for pushing me. There were many times during this project I felt lost and became sidetracked, but you were right there guiding and directing me back to the right path. I am honored to have worked with you! I would be remiss if I did not acknowledge Annetta Swift, The Ready Writer. Thank you for leading me to Ms. Paula P.

Part 1

WHERE IS GOD?

Chapter 1

SEEKING GOD

O God, thou art my God; early will I seek thee:

my soul thirsteth for thee, my flesh longeth for thee in a

dry and thirsty land, where no water is.

-Psalm 63:1

(Authorized King James Version)

"God where are You?" seems to be a valid question in times of sorrow, distress, trials, and tribulations. When times are hard the struggles of life will knock the very breath out of you. Yet, God warns us through His word in John 16:33*(Authorized King James Version)*, "in the world ye shall have tribulation." Having this warning should alert and prepare us for what is sure to come, but somehow trials and tribulations continue to knock us off our feet. I was completely knocked off my feet and I found it very hard to stand. My grief kept me down, brokenness made my heart bleed, and loneliness made my bones ache. I felt so alone, even though Isaiah 41:10 states, "Fear not; for I am with thee: be not dismayed; for I am thy God: I will strengthen thee; yea, I will uphold thee with the right hand of my righteousness." *(Authorized King James Version)*. Reading and knowing God's word DID NOT comfort me. I was hurt, afraid, weak, and confused, walking around lifeless with a bleeding heart. I was furious with God for not stopping this devastating pain. All the anger I felt was aimed directly towards Him. You see, as a teenager I always knew what I wanted for my life. I wanted to graduate high school, go to college, become a nurse, get married, have children, and someday write a book. However, my plan never included divorce. In fact it was never a thought for me. I am a believer of keeping promises and I took my marriage vows serious. Once I said, "I do", I was eagerly ready to be married until death. The biggest problem was the fact my spouse wasn't dead, yet I was plagued with grief.

I cried every day. There were tears when I woke up, tears when I cooked, tears when I showered, tears when I looked at my children, tears when I went to bed, I just couldn't stop crying. I was extremely exhausted. There were even times I couldn't get out of the bed. I was suffering, devastated, and drowning in pain.

Though I was angry at God, I still tried to pray hoping He would save me from the pain I felt. The more I prayed, the angrier I became. I was beat down. There was no life left in me. I felt as if God didn't love me. I felt alone, abandoned, and spiritually uncovered. I became withdrawn. I pushed myself away from those who had not yet discovered what I was going through. I felt so ashamed that I kept my tragedy to myself. I could not believe divorce was happening to *me*. I pleaded and pleaded with God, hoping He would cause this situation to disappear from my life as fast as it arrived. As the days passed I began to feel like Job. Everything was dying around me. My marriage was fading away, my dog died, the transmission died in the car, and a dying tree fell onto my roof. It was one thing after another. I was fed up and enough was enough!

Remembering Hebrews 11:6 AKJV which says, "He is a rewarder of them that diligently seek him". I thought maybe I should give it a try. I took the last bit of hope I had left and began to seek

Him. I changed the way I prayed. Instead of selfishly begging God to save my marriage, I began to pray sincerely from my heart. I prayed God's word back to Him. As I started focusing on His love for me, I asked Him to wrap me in His love, to hold me when I was afraid, and guide me when I could not see. I also changed my daily routine. Instead of laying in the bed all morning after taking my children to school, I forced myself to go on early morning strolls in the park. After doing this for a few days, I learned those early morning strolls gave me a feeling of peace. As I walked my brain became clearer and the noise in my head would stop. The silence in my head allowed me to be observant to God's creation that was full of life around me. In awe of nature, I would start to give adoration to God for his marvelous works- the birds, the clouds, the sun, the cool breeze and so forth. Before I knew it my mood was completely changed. With each step I would continue my prayer with praise and thanksgiving, thanking God for grace, strength, and His direction to help me navigate through my pain. My nighttime routine changed as well. Instead of drowning in my sorrow, I read scriptures, mostly from the book of Psalm (my favorite is Psalm 91) and listened to music becoming lost in His presence as I listened for His voice. Soon I realized changing my nightly routine helped me sleep and rest better. Though my tears still fell from time to time, I understood I had to do something different to get a different result. Thus, I stayed attentive to my new routine of seeking God.

Self-Check: Be Honest With Yourself

How do you seek God? (Selfishly or earnestly)

Are you angry with God? Why?

What can you do to redirect your focus?

How do you plan to seek God differently?

Pray the prayer below and meditate on 1 Peter 5:7

Father,

I long to know You in your infinite wisdom. I seek you with an open heart and I incline my ears to you. You are my Creator; you know all about me. I give you all my fears, my pain, and my anxieties as I trust you with my life. You know my beginning and my end. When I am afraid, you are my refuge. When I am sad, you are my joy. When I am weak, you are my strength. There is no other like you. I long to know You in your infinite wisdom. Cover me with your grace and fill me with the comfort of your Holy Spirit.

In Jesus' Name, Amen.

Surrendering All

After I learned to seek God earnestly, I was ready to face the storm of my life head-on. During my time with God, I repented, gaining His forgiveness, followed by continuing to read and study His word daily. I also recited affirmations continuously such as: I am enough, I am beautiful and wonderfully made, my steps are ordered by God, and I walk by faith. I had to do this EVERY DAY. Doing so strengthened me and prepared me for much needed counseling sessions. Although I was starting to feel closer to God during my personal time of seeking and worshipping Him, I still had not surrendered EVERYTHING to Him. This was the most important task. It meant I had to completely give God ALL control of my life and current situation. Surrendering was the next step before I could move forward into a pain-free life, both naturally and spiritually.

I searched and searched for a counselor, quickly becoming frustrated with the hunt. I wanted a counselor who was not connected to me due to the shame I felt, but God had a different plan. He led me to two women who were already a part of my life whom I allowed myself to be venerable with.

During my counseling sessions I vowed to give my problems to God. I promised to be honest with myself about the way I truly felt. As I opened my heart, I began to understand that some of my questions would never be answered. This was lesson number one. In other words, I had to trust the process and stop asking why. I also learned it was natural for me to be angry with God if I didn't sin in my anger. Counseling helped me sort my feelings and emotions in a healthy way. It didn't stop me from feeling them. It helped me work through them. It also taught me God was not punishing me. The pain I felt was the consequence of a breach of trust and broken promises. This pain was extreme. Having never experienced this type of pain before it drained me, sucking the life right out of me. After telling God He could have total control, some days I would take the control back by picking up the pain again. I would spiral into a sea of why questions. Totally surrendering was a struggle. I was afraid of letting go because I did not know what was coming next. I prayed, worshipped, cried, and screamed. There were days when I was silent, and other days in complete rage. I was just trying to cope, however, *Divorce was a force to be reckoned with.*

Counseling made the feelings of doom and questions of uncertainty resurface. This process was too hard. Living was a blur and I was only surviving. I hated my life and I wanted out. I remember sitting inside the car in the garage thinking to myself, "What if I put the car in drive and roll down the driveway? What would happen to me?" At that moment I really did not care. I just wanted to die.

I was tired of the pain life dealt me. But in an instant I realized I had too much to live for. My children needed me. I jerked my car into park and cried, sobbing to God again. I just could not believe my marriage was falling apart and quickly. It seemed to happen overnight. I did NOT understand. WHY? Why me? I was severely depressed, drowning daily in my sorrows. The only thing clear to me was this pain was great and *I* could not handle "*it*" on my own. So again, right there in my car I surrendered to God. I lifted my hands and said out loud, "God, I give it *ALL* to You. I cannot fix this. I take my hands off it." The "*it*" was major and would change my life forever. God took away my control, the little control I thought I had. Nothing I could say or do would change the situation. I felt helpless and displaced as my world rocked and reeled around me.

In a daze, the Word of the Lord came to me saying, "For my thoughts are not your thoughts, neither are your ways my ways" Isaiah 55:8 *(Authorized King James Version)*. Although I did not understand why God was allowing this to happen to me, this verse provided me some sense of comfort and the assurance that God was in total control. This verse made me realize I had to stop fighting against God and give up my will. I had to really trust Him with my life.

In the days ahead, as I continued to seek Him through prayer and worship, I made a conscious decision to remain in a surrendered state of mind. I did this by studying scriptures about trusting God. I stood on Isaiah 40:31, "But they that wait upon the Lord shall renew their strength; they shall mount up with wings as eagles; they shall run, and not be weary; and they shall walk, and not faint *(Authorized King James Version)*. I had to believe in my heart God was working on my behalf despite what I saw or how I felt. When the pain weighed me down, I pressed forward as I leaned on Jeremiah 29:11, "For I know the thoughts that I think toward you, saith the Lord, thoughts of peace, and not of evil, to give you an expected end *(Authorized King James Version)*." I pushed and I pressed every day, telling myself God knows what he's doing. Each day was different and though I had tear filled eyes, I was beginning to trust God's process.

Stop fighting God. Trust His plan for your life. Give your will over to Him and trust His process! When you can't see, trust Him to lead you! If you don't know your next step, move forward, trusting Him to guide you! When you stop fighting and surrender to God you will begin to see how He's working in your situation.

Release all your cares and concerns into the Lord's hands through this prayer:

Father God, in the Name of your Son Jesus, all that am, I surrender to You. My will and my way. My past, my present and my future. I let go of all my worries and concerns and I place You in control of every area of my life. Thank-you God for your guidance and direction. Where you lead me, I will follow. Keep me and comfort me during this trial. Allow me Father to react and respond with grace and love in a way that will bring you glory.

In Jesus' Name, Amen.

Self-Check: Be Honest With Yourself

Who can you consult for godly counsel?

What is your it?

Why are you holding on to it?

Why are you afraid to let it go?

What will you do to submit your will to God?

Chapter 2

LEARNING TO LET GO AND LET GOD

Finally, my brethren be strong in the Lord,

and in the power of His might.

-Ephesians 6:10

(Authorized King James Version)

As I stated before, surrendering and letting go was difficult for me. I would always pick the pain up again. Going over the situation again and again, trying to make sense of why all of this was happening to me. Thinking I should have, or I could have. Beating myself up over things I could have done better or things I should have said. These negative sabotaging thoughts would send me into a downward spiral, uncontrollable crying, and an emergency visit with my counselor. I wanted to just wave my hand and poof the pain would disappear, but that was only in the fairytale world of my mind. The thought of letting go made me anxious. Because of this, I worked closely with my counselors doing everything they told me, all while pushing through my tears. I admit, this work was hard but I had to it.

This work required me to evaluate the situation, reflect, realize who's in control, fast and pray, give God permission, and finally letting go. I'll admit it took me a while to get through these steps. There were days I cried the entire session away in my counselor's arms, but I continued to push and pressed my way. I was tired, exhausted, and emotionally drained, but I didn't give up. I urge you to not give up on yourself. Yes, it will be hard pushing through your pain, but you must fight! You're fighting for a sound mind, a forgiving heart, and happiness. Don't give up, you owe it to yourself.

Let's get started!

1. Evaluate The Situation

Take a minute to breath and focus on the present moment. Pray and ask God to move you out of His way. He knows what is best for you according to Jeremiah 29:11. Every situation God allows in your life is attached to purpose and victory.

It was during this step I realized I had to take responsibility for the parts I caused leading to my divorce. This was a hard pill for me to swallow, but I swallowed it and continued my journey through the pain.

2. Reflect and Realize Who Is Really in Control ---*Not YOU but God!*

Enter this step knowing God is indeed in control. He has over-come the world according to John 16:33. Say out loud: I am not in control of this situation. It is out of my hands." Repeat with authority and hear with open ears as these words flow out of your mouth. I am not in control of this situation. It is out of my hands! This is an important step. Without this step you will continue to defeat yourself and lose your battle.

I visited this step often as I wanted to be in control of the things that happened to me. I was hurting. I wanted to fix it but couldn't. Being both a natural caregiver and a caregiver by profession, it's hard to stand by and watch someone suffer, even if the person was me. However, I did not possess the healing power I needed to save me, thus I continued to repeat, "I am not in control of this situation. It is out of my hands."

3. Pray Without Ceasing, Incorporate Routine Fasts

One definition of divorce, defined by Google's English dictionary provided by Oxford Languages, is to separate or dissociate something from something else. Going through the phases of divorce caused me to feel uncovered and isolated. Because of this I felt disconnected from everything and everyone, not sure of where I fit in anymore. For that reason I prayed a lot and often fasted through breakfast and lunch. During my prayer time I meditated on many scriptures given to me by Godly counsel. Some of my favorite scriptures are Psalm 91, Jonah 2:7, Lamentations 3:22, Romans 15:13, Isaiah 43:1 and 41:10. These scriptures helped me stay focused as I began to find God through one of the most tragic times in my life. It wasn't that God was lost. I was blinded and deafened by the pain I felt. It was the pain of the divorce that caused me to lose sight of my faith and closed my ears to God's voice. Therefore, prayer and fasting became the tools I used to keep me attuned to the Master.

This step is a process that gets easier the more it is practiced. Once mastered   your spiritual eyes and ears will become and remain open, keeping you connected to God. With open eyes you will began to see God's hand guiding you through your pain. In time you will learn His hands not only guide you, they comfort you. Likewise with open ears you will start to hear His voice. When He speaks you will know it and not question it. His voice will warm your heart, give you security, and directions for your life.

After the Holy Spirit has cleaned out your ears- Keep them clean! You can do this through fasting and praying, positioning yourself to listen to God, not those around you, staying away from neg-ativity, keeping a positive attitude, and spending a lot of time in your secret closet away from the noises in your life. When you feel you have no one to talk to, God is there. He is always listening according to *Psalm 145:18-19.*

4.   Give Permission For God To Take Over

For God to take over, He must have permission. Give the situation to Him and leave it there. Be patient and wait. I know waiting is hard, yet it's necessary. The Lord is in control. He knows all and sees all. He knows exactly how you are feeling. Give all your problems to Him. He tells you to! Where? In Matthew 11:28

where it says, "Come to me all who are heavy ladened and I will give you rest". So rest in the Lord!

This step is easier said than done. I have a hard time waiting, so trust I get it. I wanted the pain to end immediately. I did not like to wait at all. More importantly I want to have control over things that would impact my life. I often failed this step which would lead me back to surrendering again. Repeating, "I am not in control of this situation. It is out of my hands."

5.   Let Go Completely and Wait Patiently

Letting go is easier said than done, but you must allow God to work. Trust Him with your life and the pain you are feeling. He is the Master. He formed you and knew you before you were born, *Jeremiah 1:5*. He knows where you are and how your story will end. Wait patiently for God and stay hopeful in His word. Keep a spirit of thanksgiving and an attitude of praise. For the battle is not yours it is the Lord's, so let Him fight for you, *Exodus 14:14, Deuteronomy 3:22 and 20:4*. Letting go takes discipline but it can be accomplished.

After I let go and let God, taking each day as it came, I soon started to feel a peace I could not explain. I continued to seek Him whenever I became overwhelmed with the feelings and emotions of divorce which often led me back to step three, praying and fasting.

Be kind to yourself and give yourself a little grace. Healing takes time. Learn to wait! Don't give up on yourself and don't give up on God!

How to Wait for God Patiently

- Pray! A lot!

- Praise Him for what He has already done!

- Wait in Faith with Expectation!

- Meditate on His promises!

- Psalm 18:30, 27:14,37:5, 40:1-5

- Isaiah 12:2, 30:18, 40:31, 43:1-3, 55:8-13, 61:2-3

- Habakkuk 2:3, 3:19

- Romans 8:25-28

- 1Peter 5:6-10

Self-Check: Be Honest With Yourself

What do you need to let go of?

Who do you need to let go of?

How will you let go and let God?

Part 2

Starting Over With GOD

Chapter 3

TRUSTING GOD

In the multitude of my thoughts within me thy comforts delight my soul.

-Psalm 94:19

(Authorized King James Version)

It's difficult to trust God when the walls of life are crashing down on you. Issue after issue. Problem after problem. Moving one step forward only to get snatched back what feels like five steps. Constantly feeling like you can't win for losing. Beat down and defeated by life. At least this is how I felt.

All of the above may be true for you too. Know there is hope. *Jeremiah 17:7* states, "Blessed is the man that trusteth in the Lord, and whose hope the Lord is" *(Authorized King James Version)*. Problems may seem big, God is bigger! There is simply nothing He cannot do. Whenever you begin to think he can't consider the 20th verse of Ephesians, Chapter 3, "Now unto him that is able to do exceeding abundantly above all that we ask or think, according to the power that worketh in us" *(Authorized King James Version)*. What seems too hard for you, is nothing to our God!

Take a moment to think about the power that works in you. Is it the power of God or the power of *self*? I asked myself this question many times. Most times it was the power of self, which is why I suffered for so long. Let's look at the difference between the two.

The Power of God is positive and sure despite the number of challenges that may arise. It is focused and confident and stands on the words of *Philippians 4:13* which states, "I can do all things through Christ who strengthens me". Contrary, The Power of Self is unstable and full of doubt. It is focused on the concept of "I cannot do this", or "I do not know how I am going to do that"

.... I, I, I, ...never giving thought to the Creator. Self focuses on trying to handle it on their own.

During my time of great pain, I had to increase my trust in the Lord. I realized there was no other way for me to make it through. I was stuck between a rock and a hard place. I had no other choice but to trust God. Therefore, I became best friends with my Bible. Reading, studying, meditating, and speaking the Word over my situations. Doing these things allowed me to stay focused and increased my trust in God.

You see I knew Jesus was real. I knew He was born of a virgin, died, and rose on the 3rd day. I chose Him as my Lord and Savior a long time ago. I had faith that He is, but I lost trust in Him. There is a difference. Faith is used when one believes or is devoted in something or someone. Trust is used when one has confidence or reliance in something or someone (Reference taken from Diff erenceBetween.com). To rebuild my trust in God, I had to learn to trust God again. I had to pray harder, learn to look at the bright side, believe again, and speak what I want, with the confidence in knowing it would happen. It was a process worth going through.

Here are some of the scriptures I used from the Authorized King James Version that helped me to reconstruct my faith and trust in God. For the Bible says in Hebrews 11:16, "Without faith, it is impossible to please God". Though I was grieving a failed marriage, I still wanted to please God!

1.   Trust God

Psalm 37:5, "Commit thy way unto the Lord; Trust also in him; and he shall bring *it* to pass."

Isaiah 26:4, "Trust ye in the LORD forever: for in the LORD JEHOVAH *is* everlasting strength."

2.   Pray

Psalm 55:22, "Cast thy burden upon the LORD, and he shall sustain thee: He shall never suffer the righteous be moved."

James 5:16, "Confess *your* faults one to another, and pray one for another, that ye may be healed. The effectual fervent prayer of a righteous man availeth much.

3.   Look At the Bright Side

Romans 8:28, "And we know that all things work together for good to them that love God, to them who are called according to *his* purpose."

Roman 8:31, "What shall we then say to these things? If God *be* for us, who who *can be* against us?

4.   <u>Believe Again</u>

Proverbs 3:5, "Trust in the LORD with all thine heart; and lean not unto thine own understanding."

James 1:2-4, "My brethren, count it all joy when ye fall into divers temptations; knowing *this,* that the trying of your faith worketh patience. But let patience have *her* perfect work, that ye may be perfect and entire, wanting nothing."

5.   <u>Speak What You Want</u>

Proverbs 18:21, Death and life *are* in the power of the tongue: And they that love it shall eat the fruit thereof."

Matthew 21:22, "And all things, whatsoever ye shall ask in prayer, believing, ye shall receive."

Meditating on these scriptures allowed me to see how the enemy used the pain of what I was feeling to turn me away from God. Without the reconstruction of my faith and trust in God, I would have continued to work in the power of self, going around in circles, constantly living in the pain of divorce. Don't let the enemy trick you. Study and meditate on the scriptures above.

Self-Check: Be Honest With Yourself

Do you trust God?   Yes or No

Why?

What can you do to trust God more?

Why should you trust God?

Pray this prayer when you find it hard to trust God:

God,

I love You and right now it is hard for me to trust the direction You are allowing my life to take. Lord, please help my unbelief!

In Jesus' Name, Amen.

Part 3

DELIVERANCE AND RESTORATION

Chapter 4

BREAKING FREE FROM BONDAGE

Stand fast therefore in the liberty wherewith Christ

hath made us free and be not entangled again with the yoke of bondage.

-Galatians 5:1

(Authorized King James Version)

Life has a way of making you forget who you are. I realized I became a prisoner to my pain. I was broken and hurting. The divorce caused my mouth to be silenced by guilt and shame. I was angry with God and withdrawn from the world. As I said before, divorce is a force to be reckoned with. It took everything with it. My happiness, my will to live, my joy, and my peace were all gone with my failing marriage. Divorce is a monster, but with the help of God and my counselors, I made it through.

As my spirit was lifted by the Comforter (the Holy Spirit), day after day things started getting easier. My tears dried up and I began to heal. It took a while for me to recover, but after many years I finally found my freedom. Freedom to smile, freedom to be happy, freedom to live, freedom in joy and freedom in peace.

I found my freedom in the steps listed below. By the Power of God, I promise if you follow these steps, you too will start to smile as you find your freedom.

- <u>Repent</u>

First, I repented for my anger towards God and the lack of trust in Him I displayed. This step cannot be omitted. Repentance places you back in right standing with God. Through repentance God will show you mercy. *Proverbs 28:13*

- <u>Pray Constantly</u>

Prayer became my second language. I prayed so much that even when I slept my conscience still prayed. Prayer is important. It will connect you to Christ. Pray! Pray! Pray! *1Thessolonians 5:16-18 and Jerimiah 33:3*

- <u>Seek Godly Counsel</u>

Although Christ is all we need, He will sometimes direct you to earthly counsel. Let Him lead you. He knows what you need and when you need it. If you are led by Christ for further counseling, do exactly as He instructs. Listen closely as his Spirit will show you who to confide in. "Hear counsel, and receive instruction, that thou mayest be wise in thy later end," *Proverbs 19:20 (Authorized King James Version).* I sought godly counsel and was truly made wise. Doing so allowed me to find myself again. It reminded me of the strengths I held inside and that I would make it through the pain of divorce.

- <u>Renew Your Mind</u>

Being flesh and blood we were born in sin, having no good in us, *Psalms 51:5*, but it is through the Word of God by which we are transformed, *Romans 12:2*. Renewing your mind is done by studying and learning God's Word. After applying what you learn from the scriptures to your life, you will become transformed. Transformation does not happen overnight. Keep study-ing, learning, and applying the Word of God to your life and soon you will become a new person with a renewed mind, *Ephesians 4: 22-24*. Once you become a new person in Christ you will be able to walk in the presence of evil and show the love of Christ to all people.

- <u>Forgive</u>

One will never find freedom without forgiveness. It is essential for you and all parties involved. Forgiveness is the beginning of your healing process. Without it you will not be able to move forward. Forgive even if your trespasser doesn't know they've been forgiven. For me this part was very easy. Forgiveness pours out of me like water as I tend to see the good in people no matter what they have done. No one is perfect. If Christ can forgive me, it is my duty to forgive others. I know that's not everyone's ability, yet it's necessary. Being able to forgive is the key that opens your heart, allowing you to move forward with your life. When you forgive your heart is free from malice and darkness. God's Word tells us in *Luke 17:3-4*, if thy brother trespass against thee, rebuke him; and if he repent, forgive him *(Authorized King James Version)*. Set yourself free and drop the heavy load of unforgiveness.

- <u>Speak Life</u>

The situation you are in right now may be painful and dreadful. You may feel like you're dying a slow death. Your life has drastically changed, leaving you feeling hurt, broken, awkward, empty, and lonely. While these may be facts, the truth is you can change it. *Proverbs 21:18*, tells us the power of life and death are in our tongues and that whatever you speak we will have. Many times we speak contrary to what God says about our situations. We tend to say what we see or feel, which is not what God says about us. The truth is what the Lord says. For example, if you feel lonely say "the Lord is with me", *Isaiah 41:10*. If you are sad say, "the joy of the Lord is my strength", *Nehemiah 8:10*. If you are ill say, "I am healed", *Isaiah 53:5*. If you feel broken say, "I am whole", *Colossians 2:10*. This step also helps you to use your faith as your weapon. Start today!

- <u>Sow Into Others</u>

Another way to move ahead is to learn to help others. Spend time with those who may need companionship. Volunteer your services, help at a homeless shelter, or even mentor others. There are many ways you can give to others who may be experiencing their own storms in life. Doing this will show you that your problems could be worse. It will teach you to be thankful, stopping you from complaining. Sowing into others gives you a chance to show them the love of Christ. Sow and be thankful, for you will reap what you sow, *2 Corinthians 9:6.*

- Share Your Testimony

The Bible says, "we overcome by the word of our testimony" *Revelation 12:11.* Remember to share your story. It will help others going through the same situation to overcome. Sharing your story of victory may also keep someone from giving up or committing suicide. *2 Timothy 1:8* reminds us to never be ashamed to share our testimonies as there are many looking for a reason to hold on to the little hope they have left. So, cry loud and spare not, *Isaiah 58:1.*

As you apply these steps to your life, I pray you walk in the newness of life with a newfound boldness in Christ.

Self-Check: Be Honest With Yourself

Are you in bondage? Yes or No

What's causing your bondage?

What does freedom look like for you?

How can you free yourself from bondage?

Pray this prayer:

Lord, please forgive me.

Help me apply these steps to my life as I move forward in You.

Show me God, how to forgive those who have mistreated me.

Let me love them like You love the church.

Direct me God in the way I should go.

Help me to stand still knowing You are God and in control.

Lord, I know that with You I have the victory.

I thank You Lord for healing me and delivering me from the depths of my pain.

In You I am new, I am whole, and I am complete.

I love You Lord and I appreciate Your presence in my life.

In Jesus' Name I pray, Amen.

Conclusion

Divorce is rough! It's ugly, debilitating, and emotionally draining. It caused me to experience severe feelings of isolation and rejection, which produced a major void in my heart only the Holy Spirit could fill. With His help, I was able to do the work that was required for me to heal. Day by day I sorted through all my emotions and feelings. I addressed many questions, faced unwanted answers, breathed through anxieties, and learned to walk with my head up as I transitioned from "we' to "me".

You too must do the work to defeat the sting of divorce. Pray, push, and press your way through. Remember not to quit. You can't give up on yourself. Trust your process. It takes time to heal. Your healing time won't look like anyone else's. Be patient, knowing God's Grace is sufficient for you as stated in *2 Corinthians 12:9*. If you aren't patient with you, trusting God through the process, you could find yourself in a place of depression, a place of hating God, or even back in a similar situation or worse. Your healing process is to grow you, placing you in the position of who you were destined to be, to break cycles, curses, and condemnation off others.

Be encouraged today. Know the pain of your divorce will not overtake you. I am a witness. It is because of the Holy Spirit I can love unconditionally. It is because of Him suicide did not claim my life. All honor and glory belong to the Father! Praise God for Jesus and the Holy Spirit! I declare you will live! Your heart will be healed, and you will smile again! God is there and He cares! He sees your tears, and He hears your prayers. Continue to hold fast to His promises and stand firm on His Word.

By faith I believe while you were reading and studying these pages, the Holy Spirit has met you at your very need. I pray your spiritual eyes and ears are now open. May your eyes see the hand of God at work in your life and may your ears hear His voice speaking to you.

Trust in the Lord as He keeps and comforts you every day. Wait and be strong in the Lord, remembering His timing is not your timing, *Isaiah 40:31*.

This is only the beginning of your healing process. Continue to seek God daily, and believe God for your expected end, *Jeremiah 29:11-13.*

Prayer Of Affirmation

Holy Spirit, I give my will, my plans, and my life to you! I am feeling great pain and I need your healing. My heart has been broken into pieces that only you can put back together. I need you! I am ready to receive your power to walk through this divorce with dignity, strength, and grace. Thank you Holy Spirit for healing me, for keeping me, and for comforting me. By faith I receive your divine healing.

Today I declare:

I am whole.

I am loved.

I am free.

I am covered by God's Grace.

He knows what is best for me.

I walk daily by faith.

I rest safely in His arms and because He is fighting for me, I have the VICTORY!

In Jesus' Name, Amen.

Lessons Learned

Divorce was hard! Yet it came with its own set of lessons. Here are a few nuggets of wisdom I learned from my experience with divorce:

- Selfcare. It's okay to say "No"!

- Forgive and love despite the situation.

- Stay away from people who try to give you advice using the phrase "Girl if I were you..."

- Beware of the Judas' around you! There may be more than one!

- Surrender! Yield to God's process and plans.

- Children are amazingly resilient!

- Be mindful of what you say and do! Your choices affect

others as well as yourself.

- Communication is still key!

- Breathe!

- Pray often!

- Believe in yourself!

- Keep going when it's too hard and when you feel afraid.

- Healing takes time! Don't rush it!